WHAT IF...?

For Jack, Lucy, Bethany and Carys

WHAT IF . . .?
A PICTURE CORGI BOOK 978 0 552 56519 6
First published in Great Britain by Doubleday,
an imprint of Random House Children's Publishers UK
A Random House Group Company
Doubleday edition published 2013
Picture Corgi edition published 2014

1 3 5 7 9 10 8 6 4 2

www.randomhousechildrens.co.uk
www.randomhouse.co.uk

Addresses for companies within The Random House Group Limited can be found at:
www.randomhouse.co.uk/offices.htm
THE RANDOM HOUSE GROUP Limited Reg. No. 954009
A CIP catalogue record for this book is available from the British Library.
Printed in China
The Random House Group Limited supports the Forest Stewardship Council® (FSC®), the leading
international forest-certification organisation. Our books carrying the FSC label are printed on
FSC®-certified paper. FSC is the only forest-certification scheme supported by the leading
environmental organisations, including Greenpeace. Our paper procurement policy
can be found at www.randomhouse.co.uk/environment

MIX
Paper from
responsible sources
FSC® C104723

WHAT IF...?

Anthony Browne

Picture Corgi

Joe was going to his first big party.
It was at his friend Tom's home, but
Joe had lost the invitation, so he didn't
know the house number.

"It's OK, Joe," said Mum. "Tom lives somewhere on this street. We'll find it." So they set off.

"No," said Joe.

"No!"
said Joe.

"NO!"
said Joe.

"NO!" said Joe.

"Can't you come earlier?" asked Joe. "What if it's awful?"

"You'll enjoy it," said Mum.

"I bet you won't want to come home."

"I bet I will," said Joe.

"Is this the house?" asked Mum.

"NO!" said Joe.

They had come to the end
of the street.

Then they saw it: Tom's house.

Joe didn't notice the door opening slowly ...

And Joe went in.

And Mum went home.

I hope Joe will be all right . . .
Of course he will – it's only a party!
But what if he's REALLY unhappy?

Two hours later . . .

Knock! Knock! Mum went in . . .

"Hi, Mum, I've had a GREAT time!"
"Oh good," said Mum.
"I was wondering, Joe, if you'd like
to have a party on your birthday?"

"YES, PLEASE!"
said Joe.

Some other books
by Anthony Browne